JIM ARNOSKY

EVERY AUTUMN COMES THE BEAR

G. P. Putnam's Sons

New York

Copyright © 1993 by Jim Arnosky
All rights reserved. This book, or parts thereof,
may not be reproduced in any form without permission
in writing from the publisher.
G. P. Putnam's Sons, a division of The Putnam & Grosset Group,
200 Madison Avenue, New York, NY 10016.
Published simultaneously in Canada.
Printed in the United States of America.
Designed by Colleen Flis. Text set in Horley Oldstyle.
Library of Congress Cataloging-in-Publication Data
Arnosky, Jim. Every autumn comes the bear/Jim Arnosky.   p. cm.
Summary: Every autumn a bear shows up behind the farm,
and goes through a series of routines before finding a den
among the hilltop boulders where he sleeps all winter long.
1. Bears—Juvenile fiction. [1. Bears—Fiction. 2. Hibernation—Fiction.] I. Title.
PZ10.3.A86923Ev   1993 92-30515 CIP AC [E]—dc20
ISBN 0-399-22508-0
Reprinted by arrangement with G.P. Putnam's Son,
a division of The Putnam & Grosset Group.
10 9 8 7 6 5 4 3

To Will and Betty

There is a wooded hill
behind our farm.

It is a wild and rugged place with as many rocks as trees.

Every autumn,
after the leaves have fallen,
a bear shows up.

He walks out on the cliff
where the ravens perch.

He growls into the
bobcat's lair.

The bear follows every trail, just to see where each trail leads.

He drinks cold water from the spring

and claws a tall straight tree.

The other animals hide
from the bear. But he knows
they are there.

He smells the scent of fox.

He hears a grouse bursting into flight.

When the hill is white
with snow, the bear climbs
the highest rock. He looks
out over all the treetops.

Then, searching amid
the hilltop boulders, he finds
a den and crawls inside.

Nestled there against
cold rock, with only fat
and fur to keep him warm,

he sleeps all winter long.